Families

Around the World

Clare Lewis

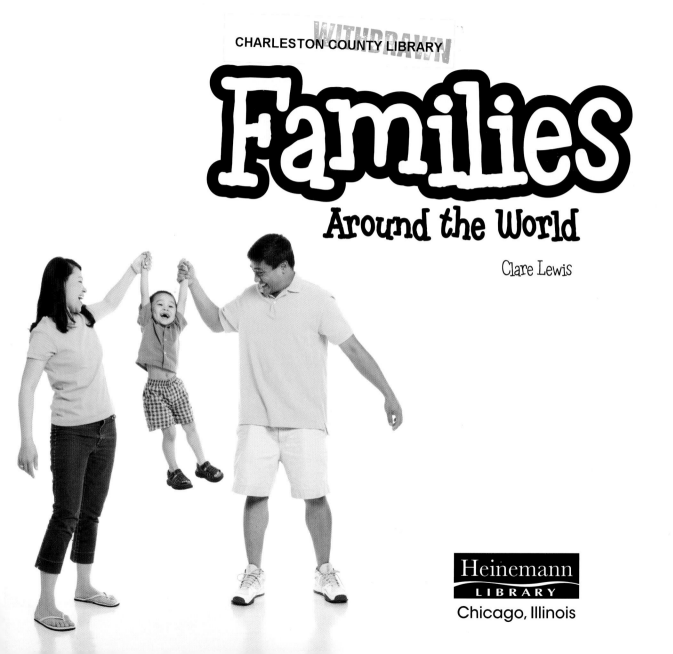

Heinemann
LIBRARY
Chicago, Illinois

Edited by Joanna Issa, Shelly Lyons, Diyan Leake, and
Helen Cox Cannons
Designed by Cynthia Akiyoshi
Original illustrations © Capstone Global Library Ltd 2014
Picture research by Elizabeth Alexander and
Tracy Cummins
Production by Victoria Fitzgerald
Originated by Capstone Global Library Ltd
Printed in the United States of America in
North Mankato, MN. 012015 008746RP

Library of Congress Cataloging-in-Publication Data
Lewis, Clare.
  Families around the world / Clare Lewis.
    pages cm.—(Around the world)
  Includes bibliographical references and index.
  ISBN 978-1-4846-0372-7 (hb)—ISBN 978-1-4846-0379-
6 (pb) 1. Families. I. Title.

HQ519.L495 2015
306.85—dc23   2013040507

Acknowledgments
We would like to thank the following for permission to
reproduce photographs: Alamy pp. 4 & 22e (both © Gavin
Hellier), 8 & 22d (both © Jake Lyell), 18 (© IndiaPicture),
19 & 22c (both © Paul Springett 06), 21 (© Design Pics
Inc.), 23 (© IndiaPicture); Corbis p. 13 (© Hill Street
Studios/Blend Images); Getty Images pp. 4, 20 & 22a (all
Wayne R Bilenduke), 7 (Hero Images), 9 (Ariel Skelley),
11 (Todd Wright), 17 (Tom Merton); Shutterstock pp. 1
& 2 (both © iofoto), 5 & 15 (both © Monkey Business
Images), 10 (© Andy Dean Photography), 12 (© Nolte
Lourens), 16 & 23 (both © spotmatik); Superstock pp. 6
(Blend Images), 14 & 22b (both Stock Connection).

Cover photograph of a playful family in front of their
house reproduced with permission of SuperStock
(Corbis). Back cover photograph reproduced with
permission of Shutterstock (© Monkey Business Images).

Every effort has been made to contact copyright holders
of material reproduced in this book. Any omissions will
be rectified in subsequent printings if notice is given to
the publisher.

All the Internet addresses (URLs) given in this book were
valid at the time of going to press. However, due to the
dynamic nature of the Internet, some addresses may
have changed, or sites may have changed or ceased to
exist since publication. While the author and publisher
regret any inconvenience this may cause readers, no
responsibility for any such changes can be accepted by
either the author or the publisher.

Contents

Families Everywhere 4

Different Types of Families . . 6

What Do Families Do? 12

Map of Families Around
   the World 22

Picture Glossary 23

Index 24

Families Everywhere

Families live all over the world.
Every family is different.

parents

grandparents

children

A family is a group of people who are related to each other.

Different Types of Families

Some families are big.

Some families are small.

Some families live together.

Some families live far apart.

Sometimes people in a family look a bit like each other.

Sometimes two families join together to make one family.

What Do Families Do?

Families take care of each other.

Families help each other.

Some families work together.

Some families play together.

Some families exercise together.

Some families take care of
pets together.

Some families celebrate
festivals together.

Some families travel together.

Families are everywhere.

Who is in your family?

Map of Families Around the World

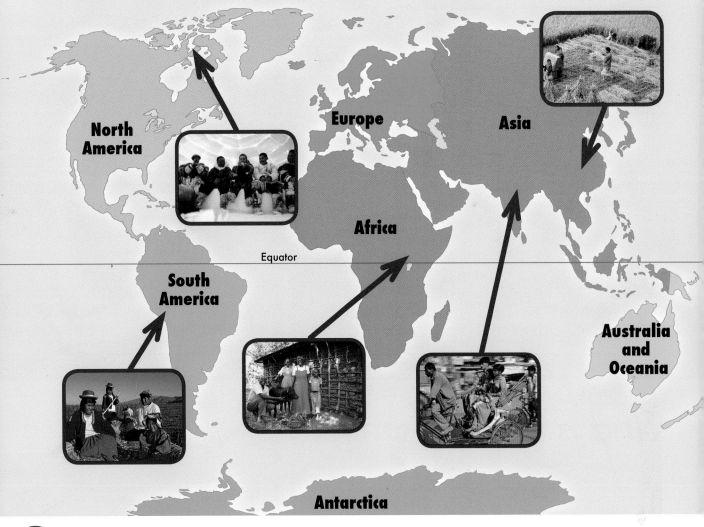

North America

Europe

Asia

Africa

Equator

South America

Australia and Oceania

Antarctica

Picture Glossary

exercise do an activity that helps you stay healthy

festival special time for a group of people

Index

children   5

exercise 16

festivals   18

grandparents   5

parents   5

pets   17

travel 19

Notes for parents and teachers
Before reading
Show children the cover of the book and read the title. Then turn to the contents page. With the children, read the entries on the contents page and explain that this is a tool to help readers know what information is in the book and where to find it. Ask children to predict what they will learn from this book after reading the table of contents.

After reading
- Turn to page 5 and discuss how labels are used with the picture to identify different members of the family. Have children name other types of family members (aunt, uncle, cousin, etc.). Then, have them draw a picture of their own family and label the family members.
- Discuss how this book has examples of families from all over the world. Discuss how there are many similarities with families, no matter where they live. Have children look at the photo on page 4. Then, point out the map on page 22. Demonstrate for children how to use the map to identify that the photo on page 4 was taken in South America.

Note on picture on pages 19 & 22: NEVER ride a bicycle without a helmet.